For Oscar and Jo

This paperback edition first published in 2010 by Andersen Press Ltd.
First published in Great Britain in 1993 by Andersen Press Ltd.,
20 Vauxhall Bridge Road, London SW1V 2SA.
Published in Australia by Random House Australia Pty.,
Level 3, 100 Pacific Highway, North Sydney, NSW 2060.
Copyright © David McKee, 1993
The rights of David McKee to be identified as the author and illustrator
of this work have been asserted by him in accordance with
the Copyright, Designs and Patents Act, 1988.
All rights reserved.
Colour separated in Switzerland by Photolitho AG, Zürich.
Printed and bound in China.

10   9   8   7   6   5   4

British Library Cataloguing in Publication Data available.

ISBN 978 1 84939 1 320 (Book People edition)
ISBN 978 1 84270 838 5 (Trade paperback edition)
ISBN 978 1 84270 837 8 (paperback and CD edition)

This book has been printed on acid-free paper

ELMER
on Stilts

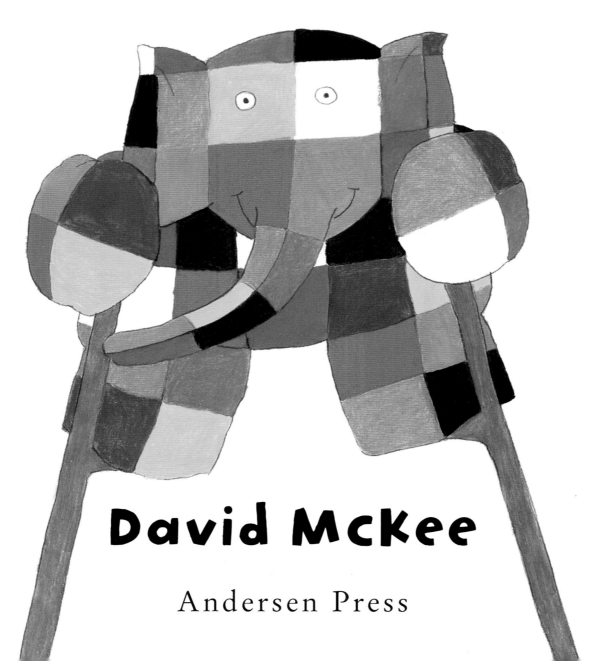

David McKee

Andersen Press

One morning,
Elmer, the patchwork
elephant, met some of his
friends. They were looking very
worried.

"Oh dear, Elmer," they said. "Those
awful elephant hunters are coming.
What can we do to escape them?"
"Hmmmm!" said Elmer. "Let me have a
think. I'm sure I can come up with something."

Elmer went for a thinking walk. He was thinking about how hunters look for elephant footprints and follow them until they find the elephants when suddenly a voice said, "Look out, Elmer! Watch where you're going." A very tall giraffe was speaking to him. "Sorry," said Elmer. "I didn't see you up there. But you've just given me a very good idea," and he hurried off to find the other elephants.

"I've an idea," said Elmer to the others.
"Let's walk around on stilts."
"This is no time for jokes, Elmer," said an
elephant. "The hunters are coming."
"I'm serious," said Elmer. "Hunters look for us
by following our footprints. They'd never look up and see us."

The elephants thought that Elmer's idea was a good one and were soon hard at work. Some made stilts from very strong wood.

Other elephants brought tree trunks and made a ramp that the elephants could walk up to get onto the stilts.

Elmer went first. He walked up the ramp, and using his front legs to hold on he put his back legs onto the stilts. "It's easy," he called. "My trunk helps me to keep my balance."

Unfortunately, because Elmer was so heavy the stilts immediately sank into the ground.
"Oh no," groaned the elephants. "It won't work."

"I know," said Elmer. "If we put flat pieces of wood on the bottom of the poles, the stilts won't sink into the ground."

"Then if we colour the stilts green," continued Elmer, "the hunters will think they are plants. We can shape the flat bits like monsters' feet. If we put them on backwards, as we walk it will look like a monster's trail, but going in the opposite direction. The hunters will follow the footprints away from us to try and find the monsters."

It wasn't long before the elephants
were walking on stilts, leaving a trail of prints
pointing away from them.
"The more the hunters look, the further they will
get away from us," chuckled Elmer.

There was one thing,
however, that Elmer had forgotten.
Elephant hunters are cowards. When they
saw the footprints, the hunters all said the
same thing.
"Oh no, monsters!" Then, shaking with fear,
they hurried off in the opposite direction –
towards the elephants and . . .

. . . CRASH!
They didn't notice the stilts and bumped right into them.

The elephants fell off, but, instead of falling onto the hard ground, they fell onto the soft, round, fat hunters.

One by one, Elmer and the elephants got up and walked away. "Dear, oh dear," they said. It was a long time before the hunters managed to crawl away, moaning. They would never come back.

"Hurrah for Elmer!" shouted the elephants. "His idea saved us. Now we don't need the stilts any more."

"We don't NEED them," smiled Elmer. "But we could have some fun on them." And that's exactly what they did.

Read more ELMER stories

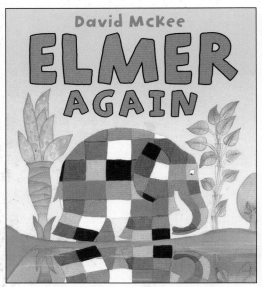

Also available as a book and CD

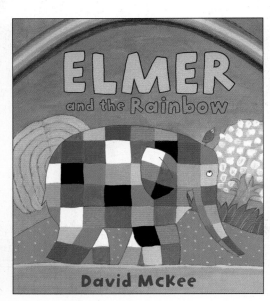

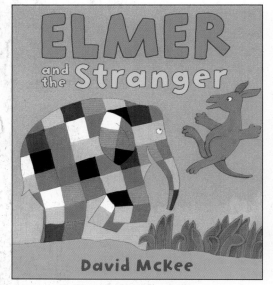

Also available as a book and CD

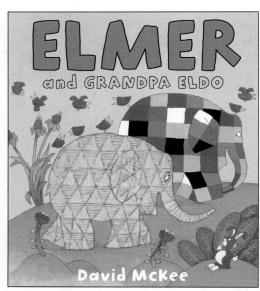

Also available as a book and CD

Find out more about David McKee and Elmer, visit:

www.andersenpress.co.uk/elmer